Austria
103

For Mr. David Oberly (1947–2009)
A great teacher is hard to find,
but very, very easy to love. You were
missed long before you were gone,
and you will be remembered forever.
A. K.

For my dear friend Judy Sue
B. K.

First edition in this format 2011

The Library of Congress has cataloged
the original hardcover edition as follows:
Kontis, Alethea.
AlphaOops! H is for Halloween / Alethea Kontis ;
illustrated by Bob Kolar. — 1st ed.
p. cm.
Summary: While putting on a Halloween
pageant, the alphabet mixes things up
with some spooky, and funny, results.
ISBN 978-0-7636-3966-2 (hardcover)
[1. Alphabet—Fiction.
2. Pageants—Fiction. 3.
Halloween—Fiction. 4. Humorous stories.]
I. Kolar, Bob, ill. II. Title. III. Title: Alpha oops!
H is for Halloween. IV. Title: H is for Halloween
PZ7.K835518Alh 2010   [E]—dc22   2009014827

ISBN 978-0-7636-5686-7 (midi hardcover)

SCP 16 15 14 13 12 11
10 9 8 7 6 5 4 3 2 1

Printed in Humen, Dongguan, China

This book was typeset in Futura and New Century Schoolbook.
The illustrations were created digitally.

Candlewick Press
99 Dover Street
Somerville, Massachusetts 02144

visit us at www.candlewick.com

Alpha Oops!

H Is for Halloween

Alethea Kontis

illustrated by
Bob Kolar

CANDLEWICK PRESS

A is for—

Ack! I'm not ready. H has top billing, make *her* go first.

Yes, ma'am. . . .

H, you're on!

But that's not the way the alphabet goes!

We need you, H. Halloween can't start with any other letter.

Okay.

H is for Halloween.

Z is for zombie.

N is for nightmare.

H   K

K is for kraken.
P is for pirate.
B is for—

But, P! That was *my* costume!

G is for goblin.

D is for devil.

U is for undead.
R is for raven.
B is for—

Oops!

Um . . . blackbird?

Goodness.

T is for trick or treat.

Q is for queasy.

Help! Nothing good starts with X!

Come with me. I've got an idea.

I is for imp.
J is for jitters.

Sorry, Jack.
J can't pick you every time.

A   D   G H I J K E

W is for witch.
A is for apple.
E is for eyeball.

F is for Frankenstein.
C is for creature.

A C D E F G H I J K L M

M is for mummy.
L is for lycanthrope.

What's a
lycanthrope?

A werewolf.

O is for ogre.
Y is for yeti.

X is for X-ray.
S is for skeleton.

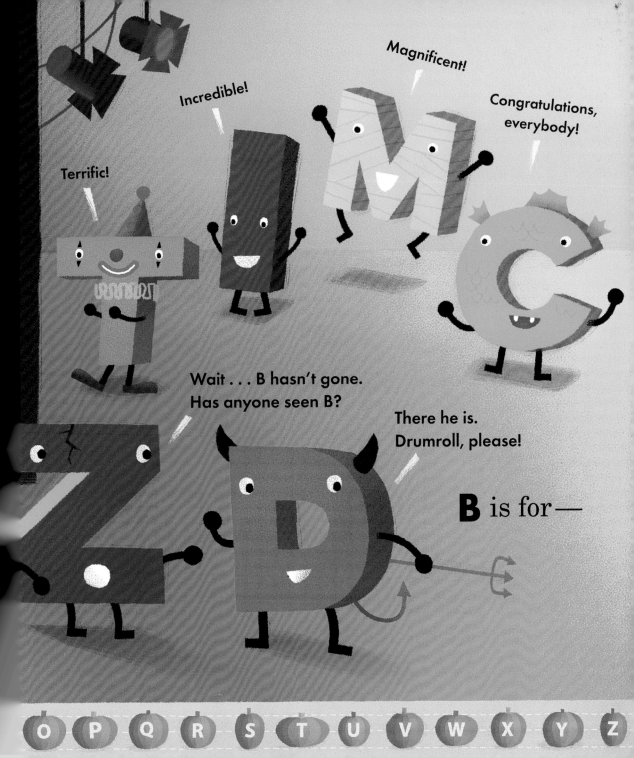

O P Q R S T U V W X Y Z

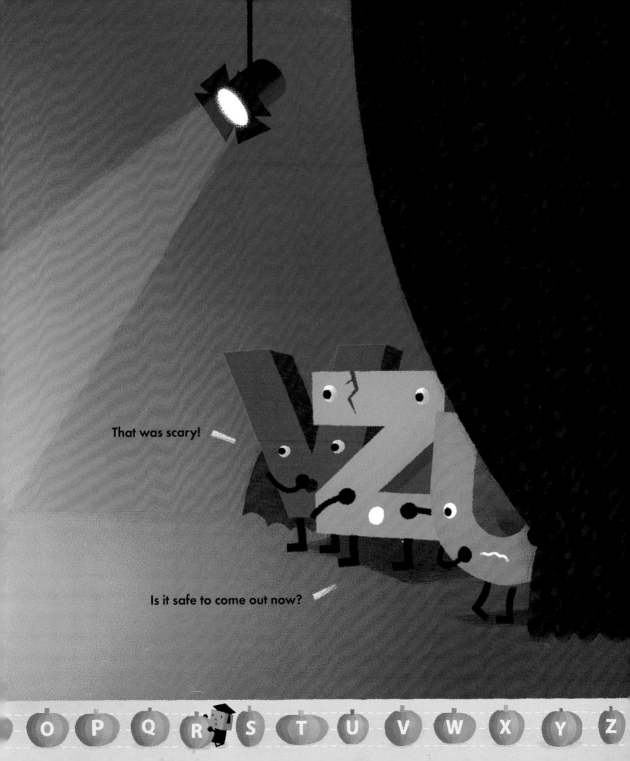

But of course!
HAPPY HALLOWEEN!

H, thank you so much.
You saved the day!

Anytime.

Hmm . . .

Hey Z, I have
an idea.